WHAT
OWEN
DIDN'T
KNOW

WHAT
OWEN
DIDN'T
KNOW

LAURENCE ENDERSEN

ISBN: 9798695587241
Published by Laurence Endersen
First Published 2020 (print and electronic)
Copyright © 2020 Laurence Endersen

Illustration and production design by Philip Barrett
www.blackshapes.com

Introduction	 9
Chapter One	Serendipity 11
Chapter Two	School 20
Chapter Three	Striving. 27
Chapter Four	Results 37
Chapter Five	Recommendations 44
Chapter Six	Romance 52
Chapter Seven	Surprise 62
Chapter Eight	Sadness 68
Chapter Nine	Safekeeping 72
Chapter Ten	Reality. 76
Chapter Eleven	Resolution. 80
Postscript	 87

In memory of Alan Murphy (3/3/1988 – 28/7/2019).

Alan was the bravest man I knew.

Introduction

What Owen Didn't Know introduces us to the lives of Rose and Owen.

There are months when nothing much happens and moments when everything changes.

It starts with a chance encounter between strangers and ends with a chance to encounter ourselves.

Chapter One
Serendipity

Her name was Rose Hilsfit.

What's in a name? More than you would think.

It is said that people with strong, short names get a better roll of the dice. If parents understood this, they might think twice before choosing sentimental names, names referring to where they first met, or some distant relative. While it's nice to honour a loved one, the child gets no choice in the matter and starts out life with their identity somewhat pre-shaped. And, in our tech-centric world, unusual names can mean lost messages and missed invitations.

Entertainers are more thoughtful with their name choices. Greta Lovisa Gustafsson took on the more phonetically pleasing Garbo. Robert Zimmerman became Bob Dylan, and Peter Hernandez emerged as Bruno Mars. Countless others have chosen clarity over sentimentality.

Rose was elegant, striking in poise and presence, with straight black hair and chestnut-brown eyes. Her parents were teachers and raised her to be warm and considerate. Though she grew up as an only child, she never lacked company. The family lived in a housing estate in

Glasnevin with lots of young families, and Rose was popular. She carried that popularity through to college, where she studied Arts. She majored in philosophy and made friends with students who shared her interest. They frequently talked late into the night debating moral and other philosophical questions.

Was it acceptable to commit a small wrong to prevent a bigger one?

What was the best use of their time here, and who got to judge that?

How far would they go to protect their family?

They liked inventing hypothetical situations to test their reasoning.

The most fun was imagining victimless crimes. What would you do if no one got hurt? No victim, no guilt. Like stealing from someone who is well insured for the loss.

Once they scratched the surface, they inevitably saw that there is no such thing as victimless. Invisibility perhaps, but victimless? You can't do just one thing. All actions have consequences, and consequences have consequences – if not now, then later.

Rose and her friends sometimes discussed whether they would opt for eternal life if it ever became possible. If they could live forever, what would be the point in living life to the full today? Is it not the inevitability of death that gives substance to life?

Occasionally their conversations strayed into more esoteric territory, like the possibility of extending time for a defined period. If they could manage this extension, what part of their life would they wish to extend? Extensions at the back end might not be fun. Extensions too early in life might not be fully appreciated, as they already lived in what looked like a world of everlasting time. They dug further into hypothetical realms. What if they could take a pill that would momentarily suspend time? What would be the best use of this suspended animation? Diving into clear blue water? A kiss? A climax?

In the real world, time knew no such sophistry, advancing on its own schedule.

The toughest debates were framed around hard choices. You can save your mother, but another person will die. They would save their mother. What if saving their mother meant many people would die? They would still save their mother. How many people would need to die before they would let their own mother pass? They didn't want to go there, as they didn't like the answer.

One night the girls argued through the night about whether they would do something truly uncivilised if they were certain no one would find out.

Though they didn't know it at the time, they were debating something that was conceived long ago, brought to popular culture in the Ring of Gyges story, which they would hear about in one of their philosophy classes some months later. The story explored whether a just person would abuse the powers of invisibility bestowed by a magical ring. How intellectual they thought they were. Others had paved the way long before. The girls began to appreciate the smart people who preceded them.

Rose was taken with the nature of time and of friendship through time. She saw that time and friendship were interdependent, though not always as contemporaneously as we would wish.

Rose wasn't religious, but if she had something resembling a bible it was Seneca's essay "On the Shortness of Life". She could quote many passages by heart. A favourite: "So you must match time's swiftness with your speed in using it, and you must drink quickly as though from a rapid stream that will not always flow." Rose had a take of her own: Things are fine, but friendship is divine. True wealth came from being able to spend time with friends; time that wouldn't be hijacked by the capricious claims of strangers.

She was drawn to both the original Stoic philosophy of virtue and its more modern invitation to accept whatever life brings.

Rose and her friends were not complete nerds though. Far from it. They enjoyed many happy hours at the college bar and walked off their hangovers in the Wicklow mountains. They talked about everything, including what they might do after college. Rose didn't need to think about what she would do. Teaching was for her.

Rose's parents were strong and rooted. They were role models in virtue and acceptance. Not long after Rose turned sixteen, she arrived home from school one evening to find them sitting at the kitchen table, staring at each other in stunned silence. Over the years, they had saved assiduously, making many personal sacrifices, so that Rose could get the best education possible. About a year earlier, one of their close friends had introduced them to a financial adviser who had been building a reputation as a savvy investor in precious metals. The financial adviser was trustworthy. Their judgement of his personal character was correct. While character is critical in finance, character without competence is costly (and competence combined with bad character is even more dangerous). This adviser was principled and well-intentioned but had no real understanding of the vagaries of commodity investing. Rose's parents lost half their life savings.

Rose still remembers that evening when her parents realised their error of judgement. It was a sombre evening, but they learned a lesson about risking what you have and need, for what you don't have and don't need.

To Rose's surprise, her parents accepted their loss without making a scene. There was time to rebuild their savings. They had each other. They had Rose. The family was healthy. They made a mistake, and it felt awful, but it wasn't the end of the world. Rose hoped she would be as strong if she ever found herself in the same situation. She felt she was resilient, but still wondered whether understanding something intellectually fully prepared one to live it emotionally.

Owen Higgins had brown hair and blue eyes. Five foot eleven, slender and wiry, Owen chose to study law and was looking forward to graduation. He had taken law despite some gentle nudging by his mother to try medicine. Squeamish around blood or the sight of open wounds, Owen preferred to play with words and thoughts. He liked to invent sayings and recast clichés. "Sew your nine stitches now" or "Slow business is no business", that kind of thing. When asked what he did to keep fit, he said that he was a linguistic gymnast, and that it was easy, certainly not "rocket surgery".

From a young age, Owen demonstrated a rare intellect and curiosity. He could read more quickly than most boys his age and liked the company of adults. One might have said he was somewhat of a child prodigy, but his parents chose to avoid any such label and treated him at whatever level he seemed up for, without making a fuss of his abilities. He grew up in Dun Laoghaire but was looking to move out of home to a place of his own once he graduated and got a full-time job.

Though Owen's mum, Angela, was an accomplished oncologist, Owen's expectations of her ability to save his dad, Frank, were unreasonable, even if they were understandable. Bone marrow cancer: a pernicious and fatal invasion against which no defences were sufficient. That was three years ago. Owen still missed his dad. Frank was a great father. He taught Owen the importance of humility, trust, and enthusiasm. Frank used to say that the future belonged to optimists. Befriend optimists. And that all of life is paradox and contrast.

Frank was a lawyer and died just a month before he was due to take early retirement on his fiftieth birthday. There are twelve months in every year, but there was no law that said Frank would see all twelve in any given year.

Owen buried himself in his college studies and in self-development, both personal and professional. He became fascinated by motivational speakers. It was as if he absorbed the spirit of his father and resolved to live the life of two people. When friends of the family met Owen, they would often hear him speak like Frank, reflecting a maturity beyond his years. Owen had two younger sisters, and they felt that he was taking on the role of provider in a show of support for their mum. Though Angela was more than capable, it was endearing to see him behave this way.

In college, Owen leaned towards the business end of his legal studies and found himself socialising with both commerce-school students and a few from his law class who were interested in how money was made. How were the great fortunes amassed? What drove people like Rockefeller, Carnegie, Ford, Buffett, and Bezos? For his final year, he chose a dual specialisation in tax law and corporation law.

Owen's choice of law was a decision made more in his head than in his heart. He had mentally divided possible careers into four main strands: (i) the money professions (lawyers, accountants, fund managers, consultants), (ii) the people professions (nurses, doctors, teachers), (iii) entrepreneurs (business-people, entertainers, artists) and (iv) everyone else.

Sure, it was a crude classification, but, as with most of his conclusions, it was meticulously considered. Each group had its merits. Owen concluded that the safest path was via the money professions. While you could get filthy rich being an entrepreneur, too many ended up poor or bust, roadkill on the competitive highway. The money professions didn't have this risk of ruin. Deep down, Owen knew that the money professions may not be as socially inclusive as the people professions, but he figured that once he got financially well-established, he could satisfy any social inclinations in due course. More importantly, he knew that with a steady career in law, he could help with the family finances, which had been severely depleted on Frank's care. Angela had also been due to retire. She and Frank were going to travel more. She postponed her retirement to help put the girls through college. With a steady job, Owen could do his part.

Rose Hilsfit didn't know Owen Higgins. They lined up patiently to receive their college degrees. It was an unlikely encounter, compliments of alphabetical serendipity.

Owen and Rose spoke for no more than a few minutes, but a lot can happen in a few minutes. Life is funny that way. There are moments that matter. Grasp them or they are gone. Smitten, and seizing this most tenuous connection of commonality, Owen asked Rose for her phone number. He said he would like to meet again so they could chat about the true things. It was a slightly odd phrase, coming from a stranger on a first meeting – *the true things*. Strange as it was, it nudged its way into Rose's consciousness. She saw a cheerful quirkiness in Owen, and he was handsome.

The graduation was a great occasion, a celebration with no agenda or expectation. It was a festivity without any impending weight of responsibility – unlike other big events, like a wedding for example. There had been some short speeches about the opportunities that lay ahead for the students and the choices they would make. One of the talks invited the students to consider what they stood for, and how most other decisions would follow more easily once that knew what they stood for. That talk bothered Owen a little, as he didn't have a ready answer. Rose, by contrast, seemed less perturbed.

Owen looked up the college website to find a photograph of Rose, which he linked to her number. Personalising contacts was a habit of his. If Owen met someone out of context, or forgot a name, it helped to have a system that might save him some embarrassment.

Once her contact details were safely stored, he put a diary entry in his calendar: "Decide when to call Rose".

Owen liked optionality.

Chapter Two
School

Securing a local teaching post straight out of college is rare. Rose got a job at St Mark's primary school for boys. Part state-funded and part privately funded, St Mark's had a charitable ethos beyond day-to-day schooling. In leaner years, the school's charitable endeavours suffered, the main one being support for single parents. The private donations were great but unpredictable.

Rose was delighted with the chance to practise what she had learned from listening to her parents over the years. They loved teaching, and their enthusiasm was infectious. They always said that if a subject isn't interesting to you, then how could it be interesting to anyone else? People learn in different ways. Her parents had long recognised that the traditional school curriculum was functional over foundational. Many cornerstone skills are addressed only partially, if at all. Capabilities like building personal resilience, asking for help, and developing a practical appreciation for how the world works.

With the energy of youth and some of her parents' conscientious genes, Rose aspired to be half the teacher her parents were. She saw teaching as a privilege that brought both responsibility and promise. It was a chance for her to spark the fires of curiosity in kids.

Rose liked the ethos at St Mark's. The teachers there were committed and caring, united in their goodwill towards the children. The first thing she noticed was a poster on the staff room wall:

> "An understanding heart is everything in a teacher, and cannot be esteemed highly enough. One looks back with appreciation to the brilliant teachers, but with gratitude to those who touched our human feeling. The curriculum is so much necessary raw material, but warmth is the vital element for the growing plant and for the soul of the child."
>
> *Carl Jung*

Rose hoped that she could contribute to the warmth and wellbeing that the school encouraged, but, as a newcomer at the school, she felt nervous about how she would be received by the teachers and the children.

As a primary school, St Mark's had more latitude to experiment with its teaching methods, unlike in secondary school, where the curriculum is tighter as children are shoehorned through state-certified exams. Rose used that latitude in every way she could. Taking her inspiration from what she had learned from the Danes, she put a big emphasis on play. The Danes have two words for play: spille for structured play, like soccer or board games, and lege for open-ended, imaginative play with no specific goal. Rose saw learning to play as a prerequisite for any balanced life. As an only child she appreciated how much joy she got from playing with the other children on her road.

Rose spent her first few weeks getting to know the children. She asked them to tell stories about themselves, to describe their favourite food, books, movies, animals, anything that might help her to get to know them better, and to allow them to make some connections on their own. How long could they sit still? There were lots of things that might look off-piste to a bureaucratic school inspector but that would help Rose bring out the best in the boys.

There were certain things that Rose wanted the children to appreciate.

- To make good friends you need to be a good friend.
- It's better to be enthusiastic than clever.
- Self-esteem is far more important than the opinions of others.
- It's fine to not know. The joy is in discovery.

The first couple of weeks were tiring and Rose was exhausted by the time Friday came round. She rested at the weekends, and thought about her graduation, how carefree things were back then. Owen hadn't phoned and she wondered why. She speculated. Maybe he was just as busy as she was, in a new role of his own. Did he accidentally lose her phone number? Did he already have a girlfriend?

At school, Rose noticed things that other less observant teachers might not. A young boy in her class, Stephen, was a diligent child and always arrived early to school. Orderly with his homework and tidy in appearance, he seemed quietly confident, yet he didn't really mix with the other boys. It was as though school was a job to do, which, to his credit, he did without fuss.

Rose learned that Stephen lived alone with his mother, Emma. His absent dad was a bad father and worse husband. An angry man, he took Emma for granted and was frequently verbally abusive, especially after alcohol. One night he left and never returned. After that, their home began to feel safe for the first time.

Emma had a job at a local homebuilder, a somewhat long bus journey from where they lived. It was an uninspiring work environment. She soldiered on. She always saw to it that Stephen had what he needed. That was her primary concern. Since her husband had left them, she vowed to give Stephen every chance in life. That started with making sure he was turned out well for school.

One Tuesday afternoon the boys at St Mark's were happily drawing soccer players after Rose asked the class to draw a picture of someone important in their lives. Stephen, however, had drawn a picture of a woman waiting alone at a bus stop, with a sign overhead that said "DELAYED". Stephen seemed sad. Rose felt something was not quite right, and wondered what he meant.

"Is everything okay Stephen?"

"I worry about my mum."

This troubled Rose. These should not be the words or worries of a boy his age. She asked him if he would pass on a message to his mum. Stephen nodded. She wrote a brief note explaining that she would like to chat about something Stephen had drawn in class. She added her phone number and put it in a sealed envelope.

"Give this to your mum. My number is on it. Ask her to call me."

Rose didn't know if she could help, but at least she would try.

A few days later a call came through.

"Hello, I'm Emma, Stephen's mum. You sent a note. Is everything alright? Did Stephen do something wrong?"

Rose put Emma's concerns to rest and asked if she could call to the school for a chat. Emma said that it would be hard for her to get to the school during the week and would prefer, if at all possible, if Rose could call to her apartment over the weekend. While it would be rare for a teacher to call to someone's home, it wasn't completely alien to Rose, as she had previously done charitable work that involved house calls with St. Vincent de Paul, and Emma seemed keen for her to call. They set a time for the following Saturday.

Emma and Stephen lived on the third floor towards the back of an apartment block which looked onto another non-descript grey building. Rose knocked a few times. The door was opened by a black-haired lady, her hair pulled back in a loose ponytail. She wore an olive-green sleeveless dress over a cleanly pressed white shirt. Her dress matched her eyes, which were the first thing Rose noticed. Green eyes, contemplative, with an intelligent gaze.

"Please come in, come in," Emma said. The front door

led directly into a dual living room/kitchenette. There were three doors off to the right-hand side, presumably a bathroom and two bedrooms. It was tiny and would not look out of place in Copenhagen or Tokyo, except that the contents and décor were old and tired. Tired and tiny, yet tidy. It was clear that Emma took pride in keeping order in whatever sphere she was in. She might not have much, but she made the best of what she had.

"Would you like a cup of coffee?"

"Yes, please. A little milk, no sugar."

As Emma attended to the coffee and searched the cupboard for some biscuits, Rose noticed a DVD player sitting on the ground alongside an old TV. There was a stack of DVDs, quite a few of which seemed to be about flying.

"Stephen loves planes, helicopters, rockets, anything to do with flying. We pick up the DVDs in charity shops."

Stephen was in his room all this time and opened his door to wave before scampering back in. Rose caught a glimpse of a narrow single bed tucked inside a small room. There was a shelf over the bed which held a collection of model planes.

"Stephen is a wonderful student. We love having him at St Mark's."

"That's nice to know. I sense there's more?"

"Well, during the week, in art class, Stephen drew a picture of you that suggested he might be worried about you."

"Worried about me? He has no need to be concerned about me."

"Sure, I understand. All I wanted to do was come by and let you know if there was anything I or the school can do to help."

Rose was careful not to talk too loudly, as was Emma, so that Stephen would not overhear.

"There is one thing you can do that would help."

"Yes, how?"

"When Stephen is not at school, he spends too much time with me. I wish there were some other people in his life, people who could help him build his confidence as he prepares for secondary school."

Rose, being the perceptive woman that she was, sensed that Emma may have been referring to the lack of a father figure. She said that she would see what she could do.

Chapter Three
Striving

Owen secured interviews with all four of the main Dublin law firms, including the one where his dad Frank worked before he died. That firm was the most reputable of the four. It respected both the letter and the spirit of the law. Frank used to say that if you play too close to the lines, the lines will blind you. Building on Frank's insight, Owen spoke of the ties that bind us and the lines that blind us.

Owen was sad that Frank was not there to help him navigate the transition from college to the workplace. He missed their conversations. While he would have liked to join his dad's firm, he changed his mind and politely cancelled the interview. He was still vulnerable and didn't want to be a person who is judged through the lens of their relationship to someone else. Better to make his own way in one of the other firms. Also, he got emotional when talking about Frank and was afraid he would let his guard down, as Frank's death would almost certainly come up in discussion.

For two of the remaining three law firms, the interviews were predictable. Owen was well prepared. He had a compelling story for why he chose each firm. This was one of his skills. His command of English gave him a versatility that more experienced professionals would do well to match. Owen was adept at reading personalities, demonstrating an endearing ability to tell people what they want to hear without compromising his message.

This skill would be needed for London-headquartered Neilson Trench. NT was the fastest growing of the international law firms that had an office in Dublin. Its can-do, business-like reputation earned it a blue-chip client base. In industry circles NT was christened "No Tears", a nod to its hard-charging style. Hourly rates were higher than at most other firms. Owen's research revealed that they completed assignments expeditiously, though some would say ruthlessly.

NT also had the youngest partners. This appealed to Owen. The shock of Frank's untimely death made Owen impatient about building his career and gaining financial independence. Given the ambitious, high-growth culture at NT, Owen felt he would need to step out of character if he wanted to turn his interview into a job offer. He decided to display the confidence of a man who gets things done.

The interview was scheduled for 10 a.m. on a Sunday. Owen, arriving at 9.45 a.m., was greeted by a mannerly receptionist who brought him through to a luxurious boardroom. At 10 a.m. exactly, a dark-haired, sharp-suited man entered the room.

"Hello, Owen. I'm Rob Perry. Welcome to NT."
Rob was tall and purposeful. Owen could tell from the intensity of Rob's stare that this interview would not be like any of the others.

The questions began, and they kept coming at an incessant rate, machine-gun style. If there was a time for improvisation, this was it.

"Why do you want to work with Neilson Trench?"

"NT is still building while your competitors are simply harvesting."

"How well can you write?"

"People will write about my writing."

"How many hours do you think you can bill in your first year?"

"As many as the top decile of your second-year cohort."

Owen couldn't quite believe that he was so gutsy, but it felt in-sync with Rob's intensity.

"Are you a perfectionist?"

"Done is better than perfect."

"Would you rather be feared or loved?"
Taking a moment, Owen borrowed from Greek literature and said that the strong do what they can and the weak suffer what they must.

"Can you recognise the devil in the detail?"

"I'll find the nub in the nuance."

"Optimistic or pessimistic?"

"My blood type is B positive."

"What separates fact from fiction?"

"Lucid articulation."

"Give me an example?"

"For a sophisticated audience, one might describe Bruce Willis as a man who has tremendous testicular fortitude and androgenetic alopecia. To others, Willis is a ballsy baldie."

Owen could see that he was connecting with Rob. He felt resonance, and his confidence was building. The questions kept on coming for about thirty minutes. Then came the final question.

"How effective are you?"

"Let me put it like this: If God had asked me to build the world, I'd have finished by Thursday. There are only two things in this life, a result and a story. I don't do stories."

Owen knew he was pushing it but felt there was enough rapport to pull it off. Just in case he came across as too cocky, he quickly added:

"I'm human, and, like everyone else, I make mistakes. Occasionally."

They progressed to the part of the interview where Owen got to ask some questions. Keeping with the theme of mistakes, and going out on something of a limb, he asked Rob about mistakes he had made over his career. Rob, without missing a beat, replied:

"Once, in 2012, when I married my first wife. The second time was in 2015, when I thought I was wrong, and I wasn't. Next question."

"Why does NT have such a large office in Milan, while most of your competitors have their European head offices in London?"

"Our head office is still in London. Milan adds style."

Owen would later learn that the Italian office was a ploy to drag certain cases into the Italian judicial system, one of the slowest and most frustrating in Europe. Useful if you wanted to drag out a defence and wear down a plaintiff.

With that, Rob stood up and handed Owen his business card.

"We'll send you a job offer before three this afternoon.

Give me your answer before nine a.m. tomorrow, Monday. If you need any longer to make up your mind, then we're probably not the firm for you. It was great to meet you. I like how you think. You could do very well here."

After leaving NT's office, Owen was buzzing. He virtually skipped home, his emotions running high, as if he had just played a sell-out concert. The interview experience had been intense and invigorating, even if he was playing a role that wasn't consistent with his true, thoughtful self. Some doubt crept in to contain his excitement, as he feared that he had set expectations that he might not be able to live up to.

A calendar reminder popped up on his phone: "Decide when to call Rose". He quickly reset the reminder to push it on twenty-four hours. There were more immediate matters to attend to.

At 2.55 p.m., Owen received an email entitled "Unconditional Employment Offer". He skimmed it quickly, read it, re-read it, and re-read it again. The contract was remarkably clear, and it didn't have the usual conditions precedent or HR weasel words. The absence of more typical conditions like personal references merely reflected the fact that NT, unknown to Owen, had done its homework on him before the interview. They made it their business to stay close to a few of the lecturers in the law faculties of the various universities. This gave them an early heads-up on the brighter students. The interview was the last step in their streamlined process, unlike others, for whom it was the first step in a tortuous one. Owen was not blind to the tactics of NT either. They chose a Sunday and a tight timeline, as they knew that he had offers from other firms. They gave him less time to be swayed towards one of their competitors.

Owen went through the employment contract one more time. It was governed by UK law rather than Irish law, but that was not unusual for a UK-headquartered firm. The starting salary was attractive and would be reviewed in six months. Twelve months was more common. He could earn a large bonus, depending on his performance. Other benefits included comprehensive health care coverage (self-insured by NT) and an attractive pension plan where NT matched employee contributions up to 8 per cent of salary. Overall, it was an excellent package written in plain English. This was refreshing and added to Owen's natural inclination to accept the offer.

Later that Sunday, Owen signed the employment contract and scanned a PDF through to Rob Perry.

Although he needed some rest, he had one more thing to do.

That Sunday evening, Rose's phone rang. She didn't recognise the number and figured it must have been one of those annoying customer surveys. She let it go to voicemail.

"Rose, its Owen, we met on graduation day. I was hoping we could meet up next weekend. Call me back on this number if that works for you. Take care."

Hearing Owen's voice was a nice surprise. Rose had wondered whether she would hear from him. She suddenly felt slightly nervous, but didn't understand why. Should she wait a day or so before calling him back? She waited a few minutes and then called him. He sounded relaxed. They set a time and place to meet. Her thoughts turned to what she would wear when they met. She chatted with her friends about it. Their suggestions were wide-ranging, from casual all the way to shock and awe.

It was a blustery Saturday afternoon. Addled weekenders wrestled with flimsy umbrellas, ducking and diving between impatient, slow-moving cars. The café, by contrast was a comforting refuge. Owen arrived a couple of hours early, reckoning he could get some work done before Rose got there.

Owen caught a glimpse of Rose as she walked by the window and in through the café door. She carried herself so gracefully. Raising his hand, he gestured toward an empty chair and offered to take her light-blue coat. She was wearing fitted jeans and a white silk blouse. Owen recalled just how striking she was. His heart rate accelerated.

Neither Owen nor Rose knew if this was a first date or something else. They began to chat over coffee. Small talk was spared as they explored all manner of things from their childhood to their experience of college.

Rose asked Owen what he meant by the true things, referring to the seed he had planted when they first met. He explained:

"Well, I guess most people go through life skating on the surface, and while that's fine, I sense there's more to explore. You struck me as someone who enjoys going deeper; a truth-seeker."

This was indeed true of Rose, but how Owen knew this was a mystery to her. Was it possible to tell that much from their brief interaction?

Their conversation was fresh, fascinating, and surprisingly fearless. They talked for hours like kindred spirits.

That time together at the café was the first of many. While Owen's work too often conspired against them, cancelling prearranged get-togethers, he always made up for it, being gentlemanly and genuinely apologetic.

Though never short of conversation, Rose and Owen were frequently stuck for time given his loyalty to NT. He would say that being conscientious was important to him. Rose felt he might have been a little too conscientious, not appreciating the trade-offs. Their chats sometimes got heated. Owen could make a coherent case for making time sacrifices now, to "buy" freedom later, while Rose forcefully made the counterpoint of what he was missing in the moment. They eventually found a way to reconcile arguments of logic and those of emotion, and began to appreciate that logic and emotion were completely different languages. Depending on the context, either or both could be right or wrong. Owen was yet again reminded of his dad's reference to all of life being contrast and paradox.

Although they had slightly different taste in movies, they liked many of the same musicians: Dylan, Springsteen, Van Morrison, Leonard Cohen. Not just the masters. They both loved to discover new artists and shared playlists on Spotify. Mondays were brightened by Spotify's "Discover Weekly", and they compared suggested compilations to see if there was any overlap.

Over the course of a few months, they grew closer. They talked, hugged, and kissed. But their physicality stopped short there. While casual sex was quite common, Rose and Owen were cautious. The stakes were higher. Neither wanted to risk a premature progression.

They regularly shared work stories and valued each

other's opinions. Owen learned about Rose's concern for Emma and her son, Stephen, and through Rose's powers of persuasion, he offered to spend some time with Stephen. This pleased Rose. True to his word, Owen followed through on his pledge. He felt for Stephen. He missed his own dad, Frank, but at least he had many fond memories of their times together. He resolved to be there for Stephen; perhaps he could be the father Stephen never really had, if he could find the time.

When Rose introduced Owen to Stephen and Emma for the first time, they quickly found common ground. As a child, Owen had played Dungeons and Dragons and loved painting the miniature characters. The child in Owen rekindled, he said he would gladly help paint any planes or helicopters that Stephen built. Though his commitment to spend time with Stephen was frequently frustrated by work pressures, he found a way to improvise. If something urgent came up at the weekend, he brought Stephen into the office, and Stephen would happily build a plane on the floor beside Owen's desk.

Time spent between Owen and Stephen was always with permission from Emma, who was delighted to see another side of Stephen develop. For the first few meetings she was nervous about letting Stephen out of her sight, but over time she trusted Owen, and found it easier to let Stephen spend time with him.

Emma saw Stephen's vocabulary expand along with the collection of model planes that were starting to crowd out their apartment. When they weren't building planes or helicopters, Owen brought Stephen to his work canteen and read stories to him about Amelia Earhart and the Wright brothers. But Owen never stayed on script. He was always switching Stephen's and Emma's names in for the hero or heroine of the day. Rose noticed Owen's linguistic influences too: Stephen's writing at school was much improved.

Chapter Four

Results

Owen's onboarding at NT was swift: a month of induction within each practice area and short placements with four NT partners. He didn't know it, but the induction was like wild animals deciding how to divvy up the prey following a kill, the kill in this case being the eleven aspiring lawyers in the latest graduate intake – each one as ambitious, as articulate, and as able as the next.

When induction ended, Owen was teamed up with Giancarlo Maisano, a gifted Italian who ran NT's taxation practice. Maisano was a star at NT, grossing the highest billable hours for six years in a row. Owen was pleased. This stroke of luck gave him a better chance of living up to his interview claim that he would be a top biller. Not content to rely on luck alone, he read everything he could on navigating a career in law. He also met a few retired partners who would be more forthcoming with the truth. The consistent message he got from his reading and conversations was that if you want to be a successful law partner, a profit-participating equity partner, you must be all-in. No ifs, no buts, no maybes.

Owen typed up a list the size of a business card, laminated it, and kept it tucked away in his wallet. It read:

> **Becoming an Equity Partner**
> 1. What interests my boss should fascinate me.
> 2. Follow, lead, or get out of the way.
> 3. Focus on billable hours.
> 4. Go all-in.

The card reflected a somewhat clinical Owen, a subtle shift from the cerebral Owen. He had seen actors get trapped in character and wondered whether he might be in danger of doing the same.

The first case assigned to Owen was an international tax dispute. It was for a precious-metal exploration company called Tristan Precious Metals Corporation, affectionately known in NT as Big George on account of the corporation's founder, an affable five-foot-eight Texan called George Murphy. George's great-grandfather was Irish. Proud of his Irish roots, he called his two kids Siobhán and Seán. Big George was a client of NT for over fifteen years and was a golden fountain of billable hours. His company amassed a small fortune from a few home runs. This was unusual in the mining industry, as explorers are congenital optimists who tend to re-invest all their free cash-flow into the next great prospect, before losing it all and having to start over – with other people's money, of course. Miners are optimists with stamina. Leveraging other people's money, or "OPM", is core to their playbook. Big George liked to call it "opium". He had optimism and stamina in spades.

Owen spent a few days reviewing the Tristan files

ahead of a scheduled Saturday morning call between Giancarlo and Big George. Grasping his first real chance to impress Giancarlo, and grafting into the early hours for three days straight, Owen immersed himself in the case files, which were like spaghetti junction on speed. To say that the group corporate structure was fiendishly complex was an understatement. Many of the names given to the subsidiaries were almost identical to the name of the holding company. Moreover, the subsidiaries were routinely renamed, then renamed again, sometimes back to their original name. The naming merry-go-round was a masterclass in legal obfuscation, designed to keep the tax authorities in the dark.

It would take more than a few days of Owen's time, no matter how smart or conscientious he was, to even begin to figure this out. Some broad patterns were clear, though. The most obvious point, amidst all the subterfuge, was that neither Tristan Precious Metals Corporation nor Big George paid any tax.

Big George received no salary. He received tax-free patent royalties from an Irish subsidiary, Precious Tristan Metals Limited, that held about a dozen patents for various mining extraction and mineral testing techniques.

By late Friday night, despite his best efforts, Owen was nowhere near deciphering the web of companies and was beginning to doubt his ability to contribute. Perhaps he knew enough to ask some good questions? Appreciating that good questions are the bedrock of tax planning, Owen decided to take an expansive tack. The Tristan discussion focussed on claiming tax deductions in two jurisdictions, known in tax circles as double-dip depreciation. The holy grail of tax planning is to get the tax liability down to zero. When it came to Owen to give his input, he asked if anyone had considered whether certain local taxes that were paid on the original purchase of mining equipment might be reclaimable. It was an astute question. Why merely reduce taxes when you can go for a refund instead? Why have your cake and eat it when you can eat the other guy's cake too? As it turned out, this was something Giancarlo had previously considered, but he liked the way Owen was thinking. Owen liked it too.

It didn't take long before Owen got another chance to demonstrate his natural aptitude. One of Tristan's offshore subsidiaries had discovered oil in the UK continental shelf and received an attractive offer to sell its interest. The taxation of profits from offshore discoveries is a complex area, governed by a network of international tax treaties. In this case the critical tax calculation was based on specific language in the relevant tax treaty, where tax was payable on any income or gains arising from the "exploration and exploitation of the seabed and subsoil".

Giancarlo had estimated that there would be a significant tax liability. Owen thought otherwise. He asked whether Tristan's subsidiary was exploring and exploiting *both* the seabed *and* the subsoil? It may have been doing some of those things, but surely not *all* of them simultaneously? The taxation legislation was ambiguous. In the relevant Tax Treaty, the word "and" should have been "or". This flaw created enough ambiguity to at least delay, and probably avoid altogether, any tax liability. Owen was developing his linguistic fluidity beyond concepts and into commerce. He had most likely just saved Big George a multi-million-dollar tax bill. It felt good and it was a defining moment in his career progression.

The management at NT immediately took note of Owen's ability, anointing him as a fast-track candidate for partner. In most firms it would take five to seven years to become a junior partner, and ten or more to make senior partner. The cycle at NT was one to two years faster, and the managing partner felt that Owen might be on his way to being their youngest partner ever. If Owen's first few months were anything to go by, he could make junior partner in just three years.

As part of Owen's fast-track process, he was quickly given responsibility for staff. Owen embraced this as a chance to develop leadership skills. And there was no harm in the fact that it would help him leverage his billable hours.

If his job was stressful, he rarely showed it. Many in his shoes would be seething at the political shenanigans of the stab-and-climb cesspits that some large law firms eventually become. Not Owen, he exuded calmness, most of the time at least. There were two areas where he could lose it. One of NT's junior associates was prone to the odd whinge. Owen disliked moaners. Fed up with the whinging, he took him aside and gave him a roasting. He also despised cynics, seeing cynicism as corrosive, the mental equivalent of passive smoking, only more insidious. Law firms, doused in adversarial DNA, conspire to increase the cynic count. For someone so allergic to cynicism, joining the legal profession must have seemed a strange choice. But Frank's words were whispering in Owen's ear again: all of life is paradox and contrast.

More constructively, Owen also recalled his dad advising that if you wanted to get the best from people you should build on their strengths, rather than try to correct weaknesses. Weakness can be coached to average, but strength can be leveraged to the moon. People are highly motivated by achievement and recognition. Give them a reputation to live up to. When staff presented their work to Owen, he always had one question for them: Is this your best work? He asked nicely, and invariably they would come back with something far better. This created a virtuous cycle, and the partners at NT soon saw that practically everything that came out of Owen's team was first-class. Everyone in his team was now working to protect and promote the reputation of the team.

Though Owen outmanoeuvred and out billed his peers, his mental recall of facts was not as sharp as some of the best in the firm. To compensate, he kept meticulous notes and a comprehensive filing system. Everything was on the cloud, which he could pull down on his phone at will. Occasionally he kept hard copies of more complex material that he could physically scribble notes on and bring home for evening study. He never brought anything confidential home.

Except once. Emails intended for Owen Hunt, a London partner at NT, occasionally found their way to Owen's inbox, compliments of the auto-complete function, a feature designed for efficiency but sometimes causing the opposite. Whenever this happened, he always called the London Owen and forwarded the email, deleting the local copy and avoiding the temptation to even start to read it. The subject matter of one stray email was "Overcharging". Owen immediately called London Owen to say that he had just forwarded an email intended for him. He confirmed that he had deleted it on his side and not read it. This was all technically true at that time.

Owen just failed to mention that before deleting it, he had printed it to read at home later, the subject matter having caught his eye.

The mail showed persistent overcharging by two partners who were still at the firm. There was a clear cover-up, and the managing partner was fully aware. Owen put it in a safe in his bedroom and tried to forget about it. This was not the time to stir up trouble. A healthy pay-check and his soaring profile at NT were at stake. Yet Owen had an uneasy feeling. Something was not right. He would need to find the right time to raise his concern. His father had often said that it's never the wrong time to do the right thing. Yet he held off raising the alarm, and soon began to worry whether his shield of honest intent was being subtly eroded by his environment.

He put another calendar reminder in his phone, this one a whole year out: "Decide whether NT is the right firm for me."

Chapter Five
Recommendations

Word of Owen's rising profile at NT made its way to the college law faculty. Twice yearly, the university invited a previous student to speak about their postgraduation experience and to offer practical guidance to final-year law students.

Owen was pleased with the chance to give back, and all the better if he could develop his profile in the process. It was a crisp, cool evening. The stars in the sky were bright, an apt metaphor for the aspiring students who also hoped to shine through in due course.

As was customary, the students were anticipating a chat about the cut and thrust of a sharp-elbowed, thriving law firm. Owen opted for a reframe. Knowing that the talk was being recorded, he figured that if he was going to give his time, he should broaden its appeal. Why craft a message for a single law class when he could address the whole world?

Sipping water from a slender glass, he glanced at the class and began:

"Some people swear by the value of positive daily affirmations. I've tried them myself, and for a while I started each day by looking in the mirror and declaring: 'I'm happy. I'm healthy. I look terrific.'

It was a private affirmation. Anyway, this daily affirming seemed to work, and like all good habits I stopped doing it. I find it hard to keep up good habits, yet I've no problem sustaining my bad ones. Why is that?

Just before coming in to speak with you this evening I was in my bathroom at home brushing my teeth. For some reason I was reminded of the value of positive affirmation. I looked in the mirror. 'I'm happy. I'm healthy. Mirrors are not what they used to be!'"

Nobody laughed and Owen saw that a few students were looking at their phones. This made him uncomfortable and a little nervous. He paused for about twenty seconds, a technique he had learned from his father; the power of silence. It seemed to work as everyone was now staring at him. He continued:

"We all see the world differently. We interpret events in our own way, and we go about our lives in our own way. How we perceive the world is governed by our default settings. We may be cheerful or cynical. Talkative or reflective. Passive or enthusiastic. Energy drainers or energisers.

You'll each have your own thoughts on your particular tendencies. We can think of our pre-dispositions as being like a thermostat. Our thermostats are set at a certain default setting, and, for the most part, we operate within a few degrees of that default.

But – and this is key – just like a thermostat, we can adjust these settings. Once you start to think about this analogy for a while, you will slowly begin to notice the default settings of others. You will see behaviour that you may not like, and then start wondering how big your own glasshouse is.

I should mention, this talk is not going to be entertaining. You may have already noticed."

The students laughed, and this put Owen at ease.

"There are a few settings where a simple adjustment can vastly improve our lives. Now you might be sceptical, and that's understandable. What I'm going to share with you is both practical and proven. For those of you who are sufficiently curious to hear me out, I will explore how changing just a few settings can really help us. These settings are accessible by everyone. They are irrefutably life-changing. They are all legal. There are three that I'll talk about. It will take us less than ten minutes.

The first default setting relates to conversation. Are you a listener or a talker? In our conversations, we can default to a lecturing lens or to a listening lens.

The rooster can crow at 142 decibels, which is like being within 100 meters of a roaring jet engine. That's almost deafening. So why doesn't the rooster deafen itself? Because when it opens its beak, it shuts off its ear canals. Sound familiar? Too many of us are roosters. Or crocodiles – all mouth, no ears.

Seneca said that one of the most beautiful qualities of true friendship is to understand and to be understood. Well, one of the nicest gifts you can give to someone is to listen to them. Really listen. Amazing things start to happen when we truly listen. When we show that we are interested in what someone has to say, we become more interesting. You become interesting by being interested. Conversations become a voyage of discovery rather than a battle of wits.

Even when we're sceptical about what someone has to say, the learning lens asks: 'In what circumstances might they be right?' Or: 'What might I be missing here?' When we wear a learning lens, we are courteous, we are focussed on bringing out the best in others, and we are never showing off how much we know.

The net effect of defaulting to the learning lens is warmer relationships and deeper understanding. Growing up in our house, there was a phrase we always heard: ABC – Always Be Curious. The curious among us prefer the learning lens over the lecturing one.

So that's default setting number one – reset your thermostat to a learning lens."

Owen stopped briefly to scan the room, make eye contact, and then took another drink of water. He could see that everyone was now fully engaged, and he relaxed further. Moving on steadily, he continued:

"The second default setting relates to how we perceive people and how we react to events. I would rather give people the benefit of the doubt, and occasionally be made a fool of, than be a cynic. Assume the best. It's good for you and it's great for the person you're getting to know. They frequently rise to your best opinion of them. I've yet to hear a good word about cynics, or closet cynics posing as realists. The kindest thing I can say about cynics is that they are not prejudicial. They distrust everything equally."

Owen noticed a few people smiling in the audience, but not everyone got the joke.

"As a default setting, it is far better in life to default

to the kindest interpretation. Most people want to do the right thing. And even when they don't do the right thing, it is usually due to circumstances beyond their control.

A few weeks ago, I was in a taxi. There's a long stretch of road where you need to be in the right lane, and we got stuck behind this car. It was virtually crawling along. Your worst kind of Sunday driver, showing no care at all for the cars behind it. The taxi driver tried to overtake it, but the other driver sped up a little as we got closer. It was infuriating. We were calling the driver names that won't be repeated here. Eventually the car turned into a hospital. It was being driven by an elderly man, clearly in distress.

I felt ashamed for being so angry. So much for defaulting to the kindest interpretation. We can extend this philosophy to adverse events. The event is the event. Any time spent getting annoyed is pointless, as we can't change what has happened.

Some people dream about winning the lottery. Now, as improbable as that is, there is at least some chance of winning the lottery. But changing the past? Zero. Zero chance. So why waste any emotional energy on it? Wishing for the impossible is just another form of lunacy. It's nuts.

Say you step in dog poo. Now that can be extremely annoying. You have a choice. Curse the poo or clean your shoe? It's a trivial example, but taking the kindest interpretation to events is simply accepting that energy spent wishing it were different is pointless. And that includes assigning blame, to others or to yourself. Would have, could have, should have. All a massive waste of energy. Clean the shoe. That'll do.

I have my own definition of stress. Stress is wrestling with reality. Guess what: Reality is as tough as nails. As soon as you accept reality, you put it in your corner. You're on the same side, and you can move forward from there.

Accept reality, and default to the kindest interpretation. A great side effect of defaulting to the kindest interpretation, especially with people, is that it reciprocates. You become more likable.

Okay, a quick recap so far. With just two tweaks to our default modes, two adjustments on our thermostat – one, trying the learning lens, and two, taking the kindest interpretation:

- We learn more.
- We improve our relationships.
- We reduce stress.
- We become more interesting.
- We are more likable.
- We help others be their best selves.

Who wouldn't want that?"

Owen paused to let everyone take in what he had just said. The students were even more engaged, so he stayed silent for a little longer, fully holding their attention. He then continued:

"Let's move to the last default setting that can vastly improve our lives. Tiny improvements forever. Let me repeat that: tiny improvements forever.

How do we know the power of constant improvement? Because this is what nature does. If you pick a fight with nature, you will learn a hard lesson. Nature can wait you out, and it's getting smarter all the time.

Let's step back. Who here sets goals? Run a 10k every Sunday, lose weight, visit relatives more often, save €1,000 for a holiday?

Now, goals are fine. But they require willpower. Goals require renewal. Once a goal lapses, we're all too often right back where we started. We're pushing a rock up a hill. Once we stop, the rock rolls back down again.

So what are we to do? Instead of focussing on goals, build habits instead. Adjusting our default settings is habit-building. Making tiny improvements forever is a habit. It is perhaps the most underrated and most powerful habit of all. Habits eat goals for breakfast.

Why tiny improvements? Because tiny improvements are accessible to all of us. Because when we continue to make tiny improvements, we are locking ourselves into a positive reinforcing feedback loop, one we can stick to.

I do press-ups every day. How many? I started with one a day two years ago. Every month, I increase the number by one. I'm now up to twenty-four per day. By my thirtieth birthday, I should be doing over a hundred press-ups daily.

The key is not to go backwards. That's the beauty of tiny improvements. Keep it simple. A simple plan executed beats a complex one contemplated. The cumulative impact of tiny improvements over a decent stretch of time is surprising, and over a lifetime it's nothing short of staggering. Compound interest works the same way.

By making time our friend, we can reduce the

incline on the hill of life, and can gently nudge the rock forwards, indefinitely. Over time the rock reaches a great height, and it doesn't take enormous willpower and effort to keep it there. We have been continually making tiny improvements, and along the way we lock in the rock.

So, there you have it. Changing just a few key default settings can make all the difference. Try the learning lens, take the kindest interpretation, and make tiny improvements forever. And remember, when you are always improving, your best days are always ahead. Now what could be better than that?

Thanks for listening. Don't worry if you missed any of what I said – the session has been recorded as a podcast. I'm happy to take any questions."

Throughout most of Owen's talk, you could have heard a pin drop. All assembled were astounded. These were not the words of someone fresh out of college. The students didn't know that Owen was something of a child prodigy, or that his dad had spent so much time encouraging and mentoring him. As Owen spoke, he could almost see the cogs turning in the students' heads. He had struck a chord. The experience reminded him of his interview with NT, only this felt better. It felt authentic and true. This was the real Owen, the one he hoped could make a difference.

Chapter Six
Romance

Owen called to Rose's house in Glasnevin. He came bearing gifts, as he had cancelled drinks the night before at short notice. Rose was unsure whether she should blame Owen or NT for the countless dates they missed. Tristan Precious Metals had been served a tax demand, and Owen had been summoned to help put out the fire. Raspberry scones and sunflowers in hand, he knocked on the door and was genuinely sorry. Rose found it hard to be upset when he apologised like this. But it still made her feel a little insecure. Did Owen really love her?

Owen's college podcast had been listened to a few thousand times which made Rose happy for him. Yet she couldn't help but register the irony of his nascent status as a motivational guru being sabotaged by his job the night before. Never mind. It was a beautiful spring day. After enjoying coffee and scones, they headed out for a walk in the nearby botanic gardens.

Wandering aimlessly along the garden pathways, they lost themselves in nature's beauty. After a leisurely hour they sat on a wooden bench facing rows of tulips that swayed in the light breeze. The sun was warm, accentuating the scent of freshly cut grass. Owen was daydreaming as he marvelled at the majesty of an oak tree. How edifying, firmly rooted, standing strongly, yet in harmony with everything around it. An oak tree gives so generously yet asks for no more than is necessary. Improving with time, its roots deepening, its shelter broadening, its splendour flourishing. He thought of Rose. She was as delicate as the tulips yet had the character of a great oak – warm yet strong, a compelling combination. He wondered what part he played in life's great garden. A bee spreading ideas? Not very noble. But helpful. Helpful will do.

After a few minutes, Rose broke the tranquillity and asked Owen why he worked so hard. He wasn't sure whether she was annoyed or inquisitive. He chose the more benign interpretation.

"I wouldn't take work so seriously if it wasn't helpful. I have a theory on why work is so worthy."

Rose raised an eyebrow. Owen had theories for everything, and she sure was curious to hear how Owen would rationalise being constantly at NT's beck and call. For a man that liked to keep his options open, it was incongruent that he would give up so much of his diary to a faceless firm.

"You know, five euros, a fiver? Well, work gives me the fivers."

Rose knew this was only the opener. It couldn't be just about the cash. Owen elaborated:

"You need your fivers, and we all know that while money can't buy us happiness, it sure as hell buys us a better class of misery. We all have core needs. Certain universal needs are deeply rooted in the human psyche. If your work is interesting and you're doing well at it, then it satisfies a surprisingly large number of our psychological needs."

Owen smiled. There was a mischievous yet endearing glint in his eye. Rose knew he wasn't finished.

"Specifically, my work at NT gives me Relevance, Rootedness, Relationships, Respect and Respite. I hadn't grasped why people become workaholics until I discovered a book called *What Makes Us Tick* by Hugh Mackay. Mackay explores ten desires that drive us. Interesting work provides at least half of them. That's when I came up with the 'five-Rs'."

"Five Rs," he repeated slowly, for effect, subtly separating the two words. Typical Owen, the linguistic gymnast at play. Taking a small black notebook from his pocket, he showed Rose a label on the cover on which he had written "Book 12" along with his name and mobile number.

"You've got twelve of these?"

Some people take pride in delayed gratification. Owen found joy in random revelation.

"I have been keeping notes of interesting things that occur to me for a while now."

"But you're pretty tech savvy. What's with the old-school pen and paper?"

"I'm not sure. I just think it's better, the way that a real book is better than the Kindle. And it doesn't need a battery."

Rose could relate to that. She loved books, including the way they felt and smelt.

"The tried and the true beats the bold and the new," added Owen, improvising from the subtitle of an investment book he had read years before.

He leafed through his notebook until he found what he was looking for and handed it to Rose.

Mackay	My Five-Rs Overlay
The desire to be useful	Relevance
The desire to belong	Rootedness
The desire to connect	Relationships
The desire to be taken seriously	Respect
The desire for my place	Respite

Rose read it carefully and pondered for a while. She got great fulfilment from her own work but had never given it too much thought. Rose saw Owen's point of view. And yet his obsession with billable hours didn't seem balanced. She thought some more, for what seemed like a long time, then looked directly at Owen and asked:

"What about love? Surely that's core to what makes us tick?"

Owen was silent. Rose had set the synapses in his brain scurrying. He took a moment to think.

"Hmm, I guess that's Romance. 'The six Rs' doesn't have the same resonance."

He was deflecting. She knew she had stirred something. She probed:

"Surely love and romance are not the same?"

She had touched a delicate subject. Owen could talk freely for hours about most things, and all day on money matters. But love – love was a big word. Love was the question with no answer.

The hairs were rising on Owen's neck. Truth is, he was falling in love. And so was Rose.

A sun shower broke through. The gardens glistened, wet with rain. They kissed in the quiet mist.

That day in the garden was the start of a new phase in Rose and Owen's relationship. They were going deeper into the true things that he had alluded to on their very first encounter. Both were acutely attuned to the difference between those people who bring energy and those who detract from it. Every time they met, they felt energised. Their conversations were vibrant yet harmonious, like birds flying in formation.

Owen was frequently taken with how Rose would do things quietly in the background, rarely if ever revealing her accomplishments. When younger, Rose learned to play the mouth organ with the dexterity of Bob Dylan, got to a green belt in karate, and was an accomplished swimmer. Owen reckoned that if Rose ever wrote a book, she would use a pen name, self-publish, and just put it out there, not caring whether anyone noticed. The simple things, the true things, the silent women who do things. Though the poet Robert Frost had written of the silent men who do things, Owen observed that women seemed far more likely to be the silent achievers.

They arrived at Owen's rented two-storey townhouse in Sandycove. It was Rose's first visit. Instead of using a key to gain entry, he tapped what looked like a five-digit code onto a small touchpad that blended in with the redbrick façade. Rose glanced inquisitively without staring.

"The cube of twenty-three," Owen confided, and in they went.

The first thing Rose noticed was the smell of fresh linen, accentuating the clean yet comfortable layout of the ground floor. They walked through an open hallway into the kitchen at the back of the house, where Owen opened a bottle of red wine.

He poured two glasses and invited Rose into the adjacent sitting room, where he proceeded to light a fire that he had prepared in advance. The townhouse was built in the sixties when open fires were the norm. Firelighters, kindling, some coal, and two logs were neatly stacked, awaiting the match that he struck to give it life. Few things are as inviting as an open fire.

Rose sat on a deep, four-seater couch that faced the fire. The fabric was a comfortable, fern-green velvet. A painting with a kaleidoscope of colour hung over the mantelpiece. Hypnotic, it complemented the colour scheme of the room. Barely visible on the bottom right hand corner were the initials "AH"; it had been painted by his mum.

Owen sat into a single wing chair beside the fireplace, so they could chat more naturally, and he could tend to the fire.

Rose asked about the combination to the front door. She was curious about where the cube of 23 came from. Owen explained how 23 was an interesting number; that most human cells have 23 pairs of chromosomes, making 23 the perfect combination generator. His lock needed a five-digit code: 23 x 23 x 23 got him to 12,167. Rose smiled, wondering: Who thinks like this?

"I appreciate this may appear odd, but it is memorable. For me, and now for you, 12,167 is an easy number to find your way back to. Remember Russell Crowe in the movie *A Beautiful Mind*? He played John Nash the mathematician who was obsessed with the number 23, and with good reason. Look up the 23 enigma on Wikipedia when you have some time to kill. Two films have been made about it. A German movie called *23* and a Jim Carrey film, *The Number 23*. The average cycle of our physical biorhythms is 23 days. I don't believe in numerological theories, but the power of linking is a great way of remembering things. Michael Jordan wore the number 23, and David Beckham switched to 23 when he joined Real Madrid."

This was the first sporting reference Rose had ever heard from Owen.

"I didn't think you were a sports fan."

Owen rarely, if ever, watched sport on TV. He was afraid of the time it would take from other things and didn't want to identify himself with some team over which he had no control.

"I'm not, but I like sporting analogies and metaphors. They make concepts more concrete."

"Jesus, Owen, lighten up!"

"Sorry. One of my less useful default settings."

"There you go again!"

"Sorry."

This was partly what attracted Rose to Owen. It's like there were two versions of him: a slightly nerdy, yet sophisticated, driven, and ambitious Owen, while beneath the bonnet lay a vulnerable, kind kid who hadn't quite found his true place in the world.

He asked if it was okay to put on some music.

"Of course."

Because they shared Spotify playlists, he knew what music she liked and had created a playlist that he knew she would enjoy. Before pressing play, he looked at her and said:

"Remember our walk in the garden when I was talking about the five Rs, and you gently pointed out what I might be missing. Well, I think about that day a lot, and this is the song that I keep coming back to."

A few seconds later she could hear a musical intro, a melodic, instrumental arrangement that introduced the distinctive voice of Van Morrison coming through in stereo through a set of Bose speakers overhead. The speakers were set into the ceiling directly above the velvet couch where Rose sat.

The Morrison song that Owen was so taken with was "In the Garden". It evoked a garden scene where the fields were wet with rain, and the singer is captivated by a rapturous creature who holds the key to her soul. This song stirred something in Owen. Rose was the most beautiful creature he had ever encountered. She had the key to his soul. And it didn't need a five-digit combination.

He took off his shoes and asked her if it was okay if he came to lie on the couch alongside her.

"Sure."

Making his way to the couch, he removed her shoes and gently lifted her legs onto the long couch. She shuffled in and he lay alongside her. They glanced in each other's eyes and could almost taste the anticipation. Before then they may have bared their souls, but not their bodies.

It started with just one touch. Intoxicating, inviting, anticipatory. Sensitive, tentative, testing for more. Electricity pulsing in the millimetres between their waiting lips as they slowly undressed each other. Blouse button for shirt button. Jeans button for jeans button. Each taking turns until they lay there in just their underwear, their bodies barely visible by the flickers of the fire emerging in sync with Van Morrison's soft tones.

Rose's shoulders were perfectly formed, her fragrance

soothing. She wore matching white underwear with an exquisite lace trim that was tastefully stitched with a single silver thread. An intricate design, beckoning to be explored in every detail.

Owen's body was lightly tanned, and, like Rose's, fit. His embrace was warm and comforting. He held Rose the way one might hold a new-born baby: delicately, tenderly, and protectively.

They kissed and caressed and explored and knew. The intimacy intensified as they removed each other's underwear, still savouring the scent on each other's skin, seduced by the threshold that would soon be crossed. And the savouring turned to rapture, until they were spent, satisfied, and secure in each other's embrace.

Rose stayed over that night. Their bond fused, each was now a part of the other. Next morning Owen offered her a change of clothes. His wardrobe was neatly organised, with dedicated places for Levi's 501s, polo shirts, and plain-coloured sweaters. A drawer for socks. A drawer for boxers. A rack for shoes and a safe. The safe was the only thing that looked out of place.

Rose took some socks, a polo shirt, and a pair of boxers and went to the bathroom to shower and change. Meanwhile Owen was preparing breakfast, scrambled eggs on toast, which was just about ready by the time Rose made her way to the kitchen.

"My polo shirt looks good on you".

Even though it was too big, it looked nice on Rose as she improvised by tying it in a bow at the back. She asked him why he needed a safe, and he explained that it was already in the house when he got there. She was free to use it if she wanted; it had the same code as the front door.

They sat together for breakfast. Things were different now. Just being together was enough. All was right with the world. This could be one of those moments that Rose would freeze in time.

Chapter Seven
Surprise

It was the Wednesday ahead of the October long weekend. Owen called to Rose to ask her to keep the following Saturday morning free. He had a surprise planned. Knowing there was no point asking what he had in store, she asked what she should wear. He had made the mistake once of inviting her to a formal event and forgetting to mention the dress code.

She thought no more about it. School was busy, and both teachers and pupils were in good form given the approaching long weekend. Rose never assigned homework on Fridays, and when it was a long weekend, she dedicated the Friday to fun activities, including extra yard time. Stephen was in especially good spirits.

On Saturday morning Owen arrived at Rose's house in Glasnevin at 8.30 a.m. She was dressed in denim jeans, with a white silk blouse and lilac cashmere V-neck.

"Good morning," said Owen, smiling, as Rose opened the door.

"How was the drive over?"

"Fine."

"Do you want to come in for a quick coffee before we head?"

"Let's hit the road, in case traffic gets heavy."

"Grand. Let me grab my things. I can't wait to see what you have planned for us."

Rose was at her happiest in these moments. Heading off, not knowing what was in store, other than the fact the Owen would always have given it a lot of thought. He didn't like to talk about love, but he did know how to make Rose feel loved. In his mind love was in the living, not the telling.

After about forty-five minutes driving along the M50 South from Glasnevin, Owen took the Cherrywood exit, eventually making their way to Dalkey village, where he parked in the church carpark.

"Dalkey?" asked Rose, slightly quizzically, as she had been there many times before.

"You'll see. Come with me."

They walked hand in hand to a café near the carpark. Owen was looking at his watch as he opened the door for Rose. They were welcomed by the comforting smell of coffee and freshly baked bread. Everything smells better on a Saturday. Immediately on entering, Rose did a double take. At a corner table was a young boy. It was Stephen, sitting there with Emma. He glanced conspiratorially at Owen, and Owen turned to Rose. Her curiosity was heightened. Stephen and his mum shuffled around their table, making space for Rose and Owen.

"Well?" asked Rose, raising a friendly eyebrow as she realised why Stephen may have been happier than normal the day before.

"I'll leave ye to it," said Emma. "I'm going to take a walk down to the sea. Have a great time, Stephen. I love you."

Emma was naturally shy, and she wanted Stephen to

spread his wings a little, build his confidence and not be spending too much time with her.

"I love you too, mum. See you later."

Every time Emma heard those words, "see you later", she had a mother's subconscious fear that she wouldn't see Stephen again. She knew it was irrational, though understandable all the same given her bond with Stephen, a bond sealed with unconditional love, the strongest seal of all.

Rose, Stephen, and Owen settled in with their preferred treats. Tea and croissant for Rose, cappuccino and sourdough toast for Owen. Stephen had a hot chocolate and a caramel slice. As Rose and Stephen began chatting, Owen was entranced by the natural warmth of their demeanour. The people profession in action, more people than profession. They enjoyed precisely an hour together when Owen announced it was time to go and that he had a surprise for them both.

The three of them walked back to the car. Before they drove off, Owen reached down to the passenger seat floor and handed back two paper bags that included sandwiches, water, and chocolate. Stephen took out the chocolate bar and tucked it away in his coat pocket.

"I'll keep this for mum."

Soon they were driving northbound along the M50. The guessing began. Neither Stephen nor Rose had the faintest idea where they were headed. It was a nice clear day, with a light breeze. Owen took the N4 exit west, towards Lucan.

Just under an hour after leaving Dalkey, they pulled into a big open space. Weston Airport.

"Okay, folks. Grab your lunch packs. That's our chopper."

Stephen turned to Rose, his eyes incredulous, bursting with excitement and disbelief. Owen had asked Stephen to come to Dalkey with his mum but hadn't told him what he had in store. Only Emma knew. She would have liked to join them but had a fear of flying. She wasn't going to let her fear get in the way of what would be a dream trip for Stephen. She trusted Rose and Owen and checked out the charter company, which was reputable and had a first-class safety record. Nevertheless, she was more anxious than usual and would be happier when he returned safely.

Owen exchanged a glance with Rose, which without having to say anything said, "I thought you'd like this."

Sitting on the tarmac was a Bell 206B Jet Ranger that Owen had chartered. The pilot, Jack, was standing alongside it and walked over to introduce himself. After some brief hellos and a thorough safety briefing, Jack turned to Stephen and said, "Any questions, young lad?"

"Does it have a Rolls Royce engine?"

"Yes – you know your choppers."

"Has it been on TV?"

"You really do know your stuff. This model was in two Bond movies and in Terminator 2."

The Jet Ranger had room for one pilot and four passengers. Owen sat on one side with his back to Jack. Rose and Stephen sat opposite, giving them the better view.

Jack explained what to expect from the journey, how long it would take and the things they would see along the way. He did a series of checks. Soon the blades were turning, and they started to rise vertically, defeating gravity, as if endowed with the power of levitation. Once they reached about fifty feet, Jack navigated the chopper forwards.

Rose was so happy for Stephen. Owen was pleased to see Rose so happy. Stephen was simply ecstatic. Having dreamt of flying someday, he never believed his first flight would be in a helicopter, or that it would come so soon, if ever. His joy amplified the natural exhilaration of flight. All three took in the bird's eye views. A change in perspective allowed them to witness a majesty that they could never appreciate up close. The chopper's rhythmic whirr replaced the daily hum and hustle. Time took on a new dimension. Down below, everything seemed slower now. Once they had seen the world from above, their view would forever skew skywards, picturing the spectacle from the skies. It was a new view, the view of the few.

The trip took them over Phoenix Park and down the east coast towards the Dublin mountains, before eventually turning west – the round trip of a lifetime. Along the way, clusters of treetops swayed in the chorus of a Mexican wave. A river resembled an artist's line on a map. People were too small to see. Earthen, green, and yellow fields formed a patchwork quilt. This was nature's domain, and it was splendid.

Rose recalled her college discussions on the nature of time. While airborne, she sensed an element of time sorcery. An hour in the air felt like a day on the ground.

Jack had been chatting throughout the trip, pointing out all the beauty spots, but he had not said anything for a while. Something seemed off. Owen called out to Jack who looked disoriented. He muttered a few words that Owen couldn't comprehend. Owen checked in with Jack again, but he was even less responsive. The helicopter started to lose its balance. Owen unbuckled his seatbelt and turned to Jack, who seemed to be gesturing to a limply hanging arm. His voice was incomprehensible. Owen leaned into the front and tried to take hold of the cyclic stick control. Everyone was terrified. Rose was calling out, asking if the pilot was okay and what was happening. Owen was frantically trying to navigate for Jack, who was not functioning. Stephen closed his eyes and held his hands up to his ears, holding his head on his lap, crouched, not wanting to witness what was about to happen. Owen turned back, held Stephen, and looked directly at Rose. She was scared and Owen could see the fear in her eyes. He said, "I love you," and she said she loved him too. Before they knew it, they were spinning towards a dense forest which became a makeshift safety blanket. Just a few seconds before, flocks of birds dispersed like fireworks on New Year's Eve.

The panic-struck noises faded to a chilling silence. In the blink of an eye, a trip of a lifetime turned into the last trip of a lifetime. Three of the four were shaken. Tragically, one was taken.

Chapter Eight
Sadness

The church was packed. Heavy with sorrow, a reservoir of tears would surely burst its fragile banks.

This was not natural. No mother should ever have to attend her son's funeral. It's simply not right to outlive our children. It's hard to imagine a plight more painful, a cruel kink in the arc of time. This was Angela's fate. First she lost Frank, and now Owen.

The priest, Father John, was a slight, sensitive, grey-haired man. One could tell that this was not his first time presiding over the premature loss of a precious soul.

As Angela sat at the front of the church, orbiting sympathisers uttered the best words they could. The circling began before the mass even started, as a handful of people arrived early to pay their respects, avoiding the crowds at the end of the funeral service. "Sorry for your loss. Sorry for your troubles. Sorry for your loss. Sorry for your loss." And on it went.

Angela and her two daughters were not really hearing the words as they shook hands with close friends, acquaintances, and people they couldn't quite place. At the centre of the tenuous threads tying everyone together was a vibrant young man in his prime. Though Owen's soul was surely nearby, it was invisible through the thicket of the collective sadness of a community laid low.

Angela and Rose understood that ceremony is part of grieving. The handshakes, single-handed, two-handed, the hugs, the hands placed on shoulders. This was human touch of a different kind. Occasionally a close friend would call it for what it is: "This is awful. I'm devastated for you. I'm so sorry and angry. Sorry."

Father John delicately guided the congregation through a spiritual celebration of Owen's life.

"Owen's time here may have been short, but it was no less impactful. He lived a life of purpose and promise and will be lovingly remembered by all who knew him."

Rose sat directly behind Angela, placing a comforting hand on her shoulder any time Angela's composure wobbled. Owen's extended family was small. The girls sat on either side of Angela, protecting her like guardian angels.

Towards the end of the ceremony, Father John invited Angela up to the altar. Carrying a few crumpled sheets of paper, she made her way to the lectern. Facing a sea of people that reflected her ocean of grief, she adjusted the microphone and steadied herself.

"Thank you for coming. For being here. Especially right now. Losing Owen is a tragedy for everyone who knew him, and it's devastating for me. At least Frank and Owen are together."

She broke down. It was too much to bear. She had a lot more that she wanted to say. Nothing could soften her sadness. Not today. Her daughters helped her back to her seat.

Father John, kindly steering the congregation's gaze away from Angela, said that Rose had asked the family if she too could pay her respects.

The last forty-eight hours had been beyond harrowing for Rose. She, Stephen, and the pilot survived the accident with minor injuries. She should be grateful, but it was hard to feel that way. Standing at the top of the church, a beacon of dignity, Rose stood upright, took a few seconds, and began.

"These last few days have been hard. In my darker moments I felt angry at Owen, which was more likely my anger at losing Owen. In my diary, I wrote:

Going after the horizon

Owen lost sight of the shore

What Owen didn't know

Is that time mattered more.

And while that may be the case, Owen was still the most knowledgeable person I ever knew.

Owen was a wordsmith. He would have been best placed to write a eulogy worthy of the wonderful man that he was. But he was more than a wordsmith. His words became deeds. Good deeds. Wherever he went, he brought energy and enthusiasm. We are all better for having spent time with Owen. It is said that some people are larger than life. Owen amplified life. He gave it light, colour and sound. With Owen's death we lost not only who he was, but who he could have been. Owen was a gentleman and a scholar, and he could have been a legend. I loved him deeply. And still do."

The reservoir of restraint that contained the congregations' grief could hold no more. The tears of some brought forth the tears of many, and the tears of many brought forth the tears of all.

A young boy stood up. It was Stephen. He raised his hand.

"Can I say something?"

This was not planned.

"Okay, yes, go ahead," said Father John tentatively.

Stephen spoke from where he stood.

"A few years ago, my dad left me. A few days ago, Owen died for me. He was the kindest of strangers. A stranger who became like the dad I always wanted. Rose said that Owen could have been a legend. Rose is wrong. Owen is a legend and he died a hero."

Mature words for a young boy, a boy who spent a lot of time listening to Owen.

Chapter Nine
Safekeeping

As the days turned to weeks, Rose and Angela tried to recover some semblance of normality. Busy days were easier. The slow days were torture. The two women became close, tethered by their shared tragedy.

Angela was dreading the thought of going to Owen's house to sort out his things. Figuring she couldn't put it off for ever, she asked if Rose would come with her.

They parked nearby and walked towards the door. Rose could hear Owen's voice in her head, gently guiding her along, the cube of twenty-three.

Crossing through the doorway was like entering another universe. It felt so strange. They moved quietly, on edge, as if they expected Owen to shout out from the kitchen. They brought some large black bags with them. Their first order of business was to gather his clothes and pass them along to a local charity shop. That would be enough for one day.

They went upstairs to the bedroom. Angela held the plastic bags open, while Rose handed out the clothes from the wardrobe. There was no protocol for this. Just muddle through. Jeans first, then the polo shirts. Rose noticed the polo shirt she wore after the first evening she stayed over. She set it aside to keep for herself. They emptied the rest of the wardrobe, and all that remained was the safe. Rose asked Angela if they should open the safe. She knew the code. Angela felt they should. Rose proceeded. 1, click, 2, click, 1, click, 6, click, 7, click.

The safe held three numbered manilla folders and nothing else.

Rose took the folders out and laid them on the bed, where Angela was sitting. Rose sat alongside her. Each folder was neatly labelled with an elastic band around it, old-school.

1. Personal
2. Planning
3. Work Stuff

They sat there motionless, not knowing what to do. Angela perked up a little, her curiosity offering some brief respite. She suggested that they go through the personal folder together. Angela would bring the other two folders home to tackle another day.

The personal folder held two documents: a double-sided single page and a few pages stapled together.

Rose's eyes were deceiving her. She looked away at first and returned her gaze.

Draft wedding speech
Rose, Today I take your hand in mine
and will never let go.
We have so much more to do together.
...

73

There was more, but Rose was too taken aback to read on. Who writes a wedding speech before they have even proposed? She thought back to how she sometimes questioned Owen's love for her, well now she knew that she shouldn't have doubted.

Angela hugged Rose tightly. She said she was so sorry, and that Owen had spoken fondly of his time with Rose. He had told Angela that Rose was the only one for him, that someday soon he would ask her to marry him and that he hoped she would agree to a short engagement, as he knew everything he needed to know.

Angela held Rose a little longer. They decided to go out for some air. They could clear their heads and come back later.

Entering Owen's house the second time was less daunting; strange, yes, just slightly easier. They went back upstairs. The open personal folder was still there on the bed. Angela picked up the stapled pages. It looked like a poem. They read it together in silence.

Life is Short
Life is Short:
    Too short for whingers and whiners
    liars and cynics
    vanity clinics

Life is short:
    Too short for pessimists
    Ark building with furrowed brow
    Dark dank creatures
    Molehill magnifiers
    You'll recognise their features
    soul shrinking, spirit sapping

Life is short:

>*Too short for envy*
>*The sin with no pleasure*
>*Clothes made to measure*
>*For grey men in grey suits*
>*Dispensing annual reviews*
>*To an army of mules*

Life is short:

>*Too short for wasting*
>*Our stale breath chasing*
>*Tomorrow's dreams of more*
>*When all that we need*
>*Is right here at the shore*

Life is short:

>*Too short for judgement*
>*Beauty might be in the eye of the beholder*
>*But truth is in the eye of the storm*
>*We Confuse contests for context*
>*Real truth forlorn*

Life is short:

>*Too short for masks*
>*Our personal brands*
>*Curated for virtual worlds*
>*Built on baseless sands*

Life is short:

>*Too short for stories*
>*So, don't tell me, please show me*
>*We get just one turn*
>*Why not make it our own?*

Rose wondered whether she had been unfair at Owen's funeral when she said he didn't know that time mattered more. Owen clearly did know, on one level at least.

Chapter Ten

Reality

Real life is testing, always probing. Mostly it's a tame test, like water finding its level. But sometimes it's a tsunami, and the landscape is remade. Losing Owen tested Rose, and it was a test of the hardest kind.

Rose had read numerous psychology books. She had studied the Stoics. But there is a deep chasm between understanding something intellectually and knowing it viscerally. That's the gap between the label and the experience. She wasn't going to magically forge advantage from adversity simply by reading about how others had done it. No amount of reading, philosophising, or indeed writing could have protected her from such an unexpected loss. Loss of friendship. Loss of love. Loss of even caring about loss.

Rose knew that one day she would lose her parents and would ultimately die herself. But she never considered the loss of one version of her future. The version where she would marry a man she loved and who loved her. Drawing from her well of learned wisdom merely spun her head into overload. Her heart and head were hurting, as if they were being sandpapered with just enough force to arrest any hope of healing.

Rose saw only darkness, and into that darkness the

black dog came barking. She spent endless days in bed, barely existing, just lying there. She got no joy from anything, and found solace only in the sleeping pills that provided some refuge from the empty hours. Taking a shower, previously one of life's simple pleasures, became a Trojan effort. A short stroll outside might as well have been a solo expedition across the Sahara. Monumental. How could this be?

Outside of a few people, conversation was impossible. Pretending to be well was too draining, the lemon already squeezed dry. Cereal for breakfast, cereal for dinner. The bowls piled up. Uneaten pieces of food solidified like concrete to build an abandoned tower of crockery. If only a typhoon could come and wash everything away. That would be better. A slate wiped clean. Start over. In the next life. A whole life, not this bare one that's filled with nothingness and false hopes.

Rose suffered for months. She confided in Angela, the person she felt was closest to understanding. They walked together. Sometimes the tears would simply arrive uninvited. Rose wondered if the well would ever run dry. "There will be better days ahead," said Angela, equally looking to convince herself. To appreciate the precious in the present she would have to grasp the nettle of mortality.

"I am broken," declared Rose, clearly still deflated and fatigued.

Angela extended her arms and held Rose's elbows so she could look her in the eye.

"Better broken than empty."

Rose repeated the works silently in her head: "better broken than empty". The exchange jolted her a little.

Emptiness seemed so desolate and barren, forsaken even. That was not who she was. A subtle change in perspective may have been stirred. A tiny glimpse of light?

It was too tiny to take hold. Rose was fragile and feared the false dawn. Shifting from a rut to a groove seemed to be a lot harder than going the other way. Rose's fall was fast. She took the elevator down. Climbing back up would have to be by the stairs, step by slow, treacherous step. She tried to show up in the world as a functioning adult, but she felt like a helpless child. Her fragile emerging confidence frequently slapped back, she wondered why she even bothered to try. This cycle of advance and retreat was wearing her down. More regress than progress.

Over time she started to get up in the mornings and even tasted her food occasionally. She pondered whether Owen would have had any theory to help her through this. He had good theories for most things. She imagined him comparing flesh wounds to mental ones, one healing in a determinate manner, the other indeterminate. Where Rose spoke of two Owens, he might have retorted that there were two Roses. Rose the beautiful flower, now wilted for the lack of water that she had cried away. And Rose the oak tree, but her leaves were gone, autumn has arrived with its short days and colder evenings. Owen could reassure Rose that the seasons change in good time. The Rose he loved would soon be restored.

Rose's mum, Grace, was of course by her side all along, nudging her forward, in tiny steps, but forward nonetheless. She encouraged her to get counselling, which Rose reluctantly agreed to do. The counselling sessions slowly worked their way towards exploring whether Rose could rediscover what mattered to her. And again, Owen's voice was there whispering, the true things. This tilt in thinking was strangely comforting.

What did Rose really want? She speculated on what anyone wanted. Some seek adventure, others safety. Some look to live large, soaking in their allotment of sunlight between the bookends of infinite darkness. A few choose the futile chase for immortality, the delusion of more heart beats than their random allocation. Others want to make a dent. Leave a legacy. Visibility in a billion haystacks. After a dozen sessions or so, a word came to Rose, yet again nudged in there from her time with Owen and his five Rs. That word was rootedness. To belong, yes, that was it, to belong. Rose longed to belong. To be rooted in life. Rooted like the oak tree that Owen knew she was. She may have lost a few branches, and temporarily all her leaves, but she could still be embroidered into this fabric that people call life, embroidered as a true colour in the infinite tapestry.

The sandpapering abated and eventually stopped. Things were clearer now. Rose's place was back at St Mark's school. That's where she belonged. She finally found the strength to return to the school and teach for a few hours. At the end of her first day back Stephen came by and said:

"Rose, you didn't smile today."

If Rose's counsellor had cracked open a door, and time oiled the hinges, then Stephen let the light in. Rose thought how the words of a child can be so revealing.

Rose's soul softened. Time is subtle. She may have seen suffering and indiscriminate loss at the individual level, but humanity marched on regardless. If she could just hang in there with humanity, she could march on with it, taking time and tides as they come.

Chapter Eleven
Resolution

However tough Rose's situation was, there was always someone carrying a heavier load.

Angela had her own grief to work through. She had previously found a road map to come through Frank's death. Irrespective of the terrain, there is always a way through. Eventually.

Picking up the folder labelled "Planning", Angela removed the elastic band. Inside was a collection of newspaper clippings about helicopter tours, leadership, the profits of the largest law firms, honeymoon destinations, and an article about The Giving Pledge. The Giving Pledge was founded by Warren Buffett and Bill Gates. The idea was to encourage wealthy individuals to commit to giving up most of their wealth to philanthropic causes while they were still alive. It was genius in its simplicity, scope, and impact. Angela could see why Owen would have been intrigued.

The folder also had an official-looking document with a binding down its side. She took a closer look. A will? Owen had a will? Surprising for such a young person, but not so unusual for a lawyer, she supposed. Not that Owen would have accumulated much, or anything at all. He had a decent salary, but he died young and his house was rented.

Angela leafed through to the clause that read:

"I hereby direct that the entirety of my estate be given over to St Mark's School, Glasnevin, Dublin for its own use absolutely."

Angela allowed herself a smile, the reassuring smile of a proud mother. Owen, her son Owen, was good. Angela knew all about the great work at St Mark's from her conversations with Rose, and that any funds, no matter how small, could be put to exceptionally good use there. Whatever resources Owen had, Angela would help assemble what she could. The process should not be too onerous, as Owen had appointed Angela and a co-worker of her late husband Frank, as executors. Frank's previous co-worker, Justin, was still practising as a legal partner at the practice where Frank had worked and was a trusted family friend. Angela found a bank statement with a cash balance of roughly eleven thousand euros, which was a lot given that Owen wasn't working that long. The motivation of the cause got her thinking. Owen had mentioned something about generous health coverage. When Frank died, the family house mortgage was paid off from the proceeds of an insurance policy that the bank insisted be taken out when they bought the house. Perhaps Owen's contract had something similar.

Angela reached for the third folder, "Work Stuff", the thickest of the three. Owens employment contract was the first thing in there, sitting on top. Angela skimmed through it. And yes, there it was, death-in-service benefit. Five times annual salary. Now *that* would make a difference.

First thing next morning, Angela rang the main office number at NT and asked to speak to someone in HR. The HR contact was courteous and expressed his condolences. Angela was invited to come into the office so they could go through everything in person.

I can see why Owen liked working here, Angela thought to herself as she sat in NT's reception taking in the wonderful views and bustling atmosphere. After a twenty-minute wait, she was shown to the main boardroom, a spacious room with a long mahogany table. A man was waiting at the door.

"Hi, I'm Rob Perry. You may not remember me, but we met briefly at Owen's funeral. He was a great lawyer and a conscientious colleague. I'm really sorry for your loss."

Rob asked Angela to take a seat. She was confused. There were three men and three women seated at the other side of the table. Why so many people? A gentleman in a white shirt and black waistcoat offered refreshments. Angela asked for still water.

One of the female lawyers started talking. She expressed her condolences and then said there was a problem with Owen's death-in-service claim. Angela was surprised but listened patiently. A third lawyer stood up and handed out a copy of Owen's employment contract.

"Owen's death in service is not valid. We have highlighted the relevant clause on page three. Owen died during a high-risk activity. Those activities are only covered if the firm is notified in advance. Owen never notified us."

The lawyer's tone was formal. Angela said that she

didn't understand how the claim could be invalid. Owen was always very conscientious about these things, and if he somehow failed to advise of the helicopter trip, it would have been unintentional. Keeping her cool, she said she would have to get independent legal advice.

NT's reaction was calculated and designed to be somewhat threatening. Not directly – they were too smart for that – but threatening in a passive-aggressive way. They explained how any legal process would be drawn out and very expensive. It may even end up in the Italian courts, as the insurance company that wrote the death-in-service cover was based there.

Unbowed, Angela stood up and left without saying anything. As she was leaving the room, she turned and looked directly at Rob Perry. She didn't need to say anything; her expression clearly indicated that this wasn't over.

While Angela was at NT, Justin, the other executor of the will, had been going through Owen's work files. Angela probably should have brought him along to the NT meeting, but she wasn't expecting to be stonewalled. Justin had some news for her. He had found an email from Owen to NT clearly advising of his plan to take a helicopter tour, and an acknowledgement from NT's head of HR. There was more. NT was overcharging its clients.

This both angered and pleased Angela: she was angry at the deception but pleased that Owen's wishes for St Mark's might be respected after all. But one thing still bothered her. Why would NT resist the claim if they were insured? Justin explained what was going on. While most firms use external insurers, on rare occasions some firms opted to self-insure, by setting up an internal fund. NT had chosen this route, and its internal fund was based in Italy. Any proceeds would essentially be coming from their pocket. That explained a lot.

Justin laid out his plan of action. First, he would extract an acknowledgement that the death-in-service claim was valid. Second, when NT had accepted, in writing, the unconditional validity of the death in service claim, then, and only then, would he raise the issue of overcharging. Third, he would expose NT's wrongdoing. There should be consequences. Treachery is borrowed from the truth, and eventually the truth comes looking for payment.

Justin said that Angela should not worry about the legal costs, for two reasons. Firstly, out of respect for Frank, who he had worked closely with for almost fifteen years, Justin wanted to take the case through the main first phase on a pro-bono basis. Secondly, if NT tried to drag the case out, Angela could access financing from a third party through a product called litigation finance. The litigation finance provider would finance the case and take a share of any settlement. If the case failed, Angela wouldn't be out of pocket. For technical reasons, this external financing option was only available because Owen's contract was governed by UK law.

Justin's first order of business was to serve a notice of discovery seeking all the emails that Owen had sent over the time leading up to the accident. After some wrangling, NT eventually "found" the helicopter notice email and claimed that they originally missed it due to an administrative oversight caused by an IT malfunction. They acknowledged that their decision to deny the death-in-service claim was wrong. Owen's total annual compensation including salary and bonus would have been €100,000, which meant a death in service claim of €500,000. Justin pressed that NT's claim of an administrative error was highly suspect and that they were negligent in their duty of care to Angela. NT eventually settled for €1 million, which duly worked through probate to be paid over to St Mark's as directed in Owen's will.

Once the probate funds cleared, Justin raised the overcharging issue simultaneously with NT and the Law Society of Ireland. Months later, Angela would read in the paper that NT was sanctioned and that three partners, including its managing partner, had resigned, pending criminal proceedings.

Rose took a phone call from Angela, who said that she had something Rose should see. Rose asked what it was, but Angela suggested it would be better if they met in person. They agreed that Rose would call to Angela's house that evening.

Angela welcomed Rose and they went through to the kitchen. As they sat around the table, Angela took Rose through her entire experience with NT including the deception and the overcharging.

Rose listened dutifully but wondered where this was leading. There was a short gap in conversation. Angela went to a kitchen drawer and took out an envelope. She opened it and slid a bank draft across the table in Rose's direction.

"Please pay to the order of:
The board of trustees of St Mark's School

One Million Euros only."

Rose froze and didn't feel the tears as they trickled down her face. Maybe all was okay with the world. It's a virtuous cycle. The leaves die and fall away. But spring always returns, building on the winter that has cleared the way. Rose was looking at Angela and thinking of Owen.

What's in a name? Her name was Rose Hilsfit. The answer was there all along.

Life is short.

Rose had so much left to do. Owen knew.

Postscript

Owen's autopsy was sitting on Angela's growing pile of paperwork. It was needed for the legal case, but she hadn't read it in detail. The cause of the accident was clear: pilot error. Jack had suffered a mild stroke and lost control. Owen's cause of death was also clear: a broken neck on impact. But what Angela hadn't known was that from the nature of the injury, it seemed highly likely that Owen had used his body to protect Stephen in those last few fatal seconds. Stephen was right when he said that Owen died for him.

With the additional funds now available to St Mark's, they were able to bring on some more help to assist with its charitable endeavours. This included creating a new post that was offered to Stephen's mother, Emma, which she gladly accepted and in which she flourished.

Stephen came out of his shell and moved to secondary school, where he became part of a tightly knit group of friends. He had, after all, survived a helicopter crash and his friends thought that was awesome. He still missed Owen.

As for Rose, we don't know. Rose's story was still unfolding, like a flower in springtime.

There is so much we don't know, can't know, and will

never know.

But there is one thing we do know.

We know that time matters most.

About the Author

Laurence Endersen lives with his family in Dublin, Ireland.

What Owen Didn't Know is his second book.

Also by Laurence:
Pebbles of Perception: How A Few Good Choices Make All the Difference

Acknowledgements

Thank you to Angela Brennan, Anne Marie Curtin, Barry Brennan, Brent Beshore, Brian O'Kelly, Cathal Carroll, Ciara Murphy, David Jameson, David O'Flynn, David Ornstein, Emer Kennedy, Fiona Endersen, Henning Kielhorn, Jonathan Escott, John Forde, John Jeffery, John O'Brien, Jeff Annello, Kathy Endersen, Kevin Harmon, Kris Powell, Laurence J Endersen, Lisa McCarthy, Louise Endersen, Michelle Endersen (who gently helped restore the balance between thinking and feeling), Niall O'Sullivan, Paul Ciampa, Paul McCarthy, Paul McMillan, Paul Reidy, Philip Barrett, Ray McMahon, Ronan O'Houlihan, Sarah Endersen, Sarah O'Grady, Shane Parrish, Stan Carey, Stefan Jibodh, Valerie O'Flynn, and Yolanda Healy.

You each gave generously of your time and encouragement. Rose and Owen's story is all the better for your thoughtful contributions, and mine is so much better for your friendship.

The following pages leave some space for your own reflections.

What would I do if I wasn't afraid?

....
....
....
....
....
....
....
....
....
....
....
....
....
....
....
....
....
....
....
....
....
....
....
....

Who should I spend more time with?

....
....
....
....
....
....
....
....
....
....
....
....
....
....
....
....
....
....
....
....
....
....
....
....
....

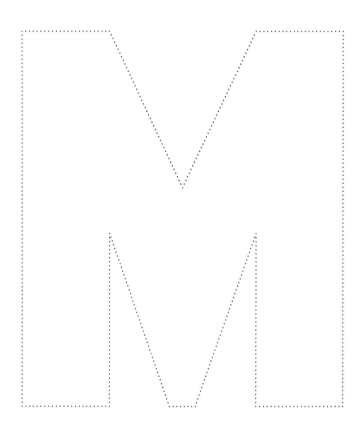

How do I make more of my time my own?

....
....
....
....
....
....
....
....
....
....
....
....
....
....
....
....
....
....
....
....
....
....
....
....
....

Concluding thoughts…

....
....
....
....
....
....
....
....
....
....
....
....
....
....
....
....
....
....
....
....
....
....
....
....
....

Printed in Poland
by Amazon Fulfillment
Poland Sp. z o.o., Wrocław

63710778R00061